A TALE OF TWO BEASTS

FIONA ROBERTON

Hodder
Children's
Books

FOR DAVID
THERE ARE TWO SIDES
TO EVERY STORY,
AND THEN THERE
IS THE TRUTH.
MARK TWAIN

THE
DEEP DARK WOODS

WAY OUT →

← PICNIC AREA

feep

feep

I was walking home from Grandma's
house, through the deep dark woods,
when I spied a strange little beast.

He was stuck up a tree,
and whining sadly...

FEEP!

...so I decided to rescue him.

"I will call you Fang!"
I told him,

and I wrapped him
warmly up in my scarf,

and carried him safely home.

I gave him a lovely bath,

and a gorgeous new hat and jumper,

and a delicious
bowl of fresh nuts.

I made him a beautiful
house, and gave him
Lord Rex to play with.

I took him out for lots of long walkies...

to keep him fit...

and healthy.

And I showed him off to ALL my friends,
who loved him nearly as much as I did.

But for some strange reason,
the little beast did not look
very happy.

In fact, he was looking rather hot.
'I hope he's not sick,' I thought...

...and opened the window
to cool him down.

But then something
TERRIBLE happened!

He threw off his clothes,
leapt out of the window...

FANG!

FEEP!

...and ran away as fast as he could,
back to the deep dark woods.

I wanted to go and look for him,
but Mama had other plans.

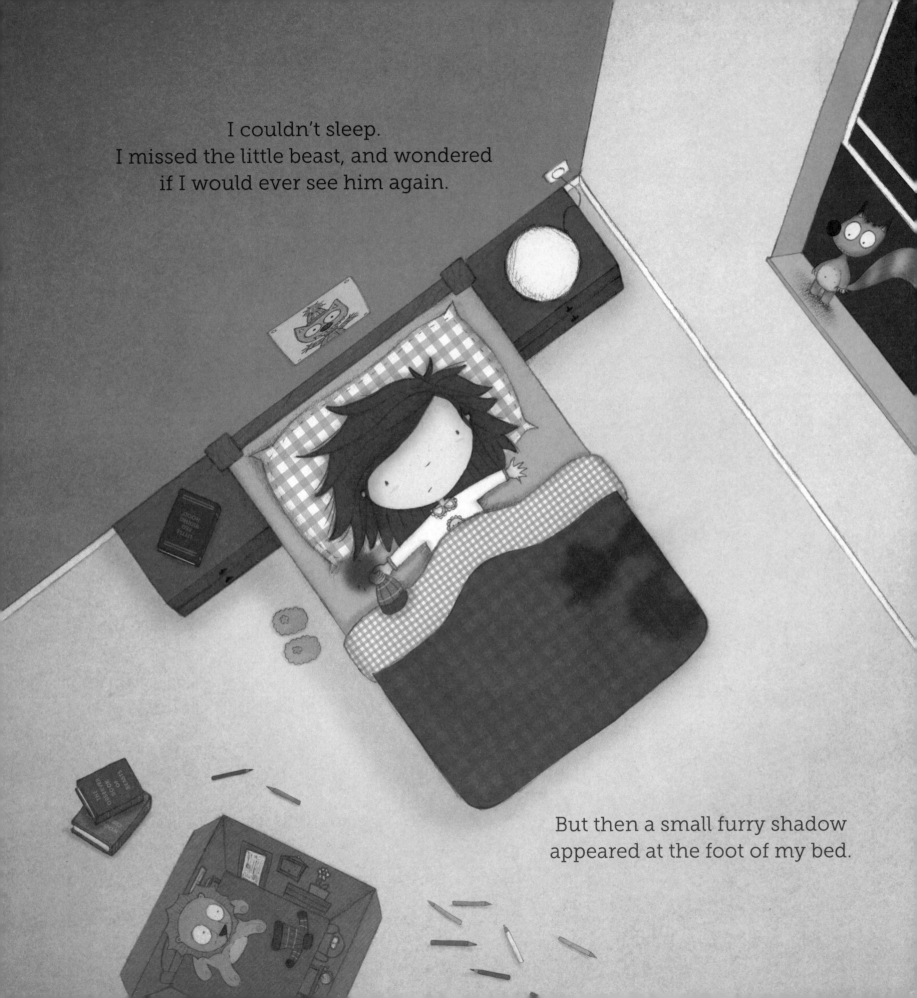

I couldn't sleep.
I missed the little beast, and wondered
if I would ever see him again.

But then a small furry shadow
appeared at the foot of my bed.

The strange little
beast had returned.

He seemed quite
pleased to see me,

and I began to think that
maybe, just maybe...

...he wasn't that strange after all.

I wonder why he came back?

A TALE OF TWO BEASTS

PART TWO

THE
TERRIBLE
BEAST

FIONA ROBERTON

FOR DAVID
IT WAS THE BEST
OF TIMES,
IT WAS THE WORST
OF TIMES.

CHARLES DICKENS

tra la la la

tra la la la

THE
DEEP DARK WOODS
WAY OUT →
← PICNIC AREA

I was hanging from my
favourite tree, singing
happily to the birds when...

HEY!

...I was
AMBUSHED
by a terrible beast!

GROWF!

She growled at me,

and tied me up,

and carried me off
to her secret lair.

She made me
disgustingly clean,

and dressed me up in a
ridiculous hat and jumper,

and tried to make me
eat squirrel food.

She kept me in a tiny box, with nothing for me to do and nowhere for me to hang from.

She made me walk backwards...

and forwards...

and backwards again,
for no reason what-so-ever.

She showed me off to a herd of
even wilder beasts, who were just
as terrible as she was.

FREE ONCE MORE!

I raced back to the deep dark woods,
before the terrible beast could catch me.

It was peaceful in the
deep dark woods,

a bit too peaceful perhaps.

And also, a bit wet.

In weather like this one could
do with a nice warm hat.

I snuck back to retrieve it
under cover of darkness.

The terrible beast
was waiting for me.

She seemed quite
pleased to see me,

and I began to think that
maybe, just maybe...

...she wasn't that terrible after all.

First published in 2015 by Hodder Children's Books

This edition published in 2016

Hodder Children's Books

An imprint of Hachette Children's Group

Part of Hodder & Stoughton, Carmelite House, 50 Victoria Embankment, London EC4Y 0DZ

A catalogue record of this book is available from the British Library.

ISBN: 978 1 444 91673 7

10 9 8 7 6 5 4 3 2 1

Printed in China

An Hachette UK Company

www.hachette.co.uk